STEAKING A CLAIM

IRON & FLAME COZY MYSTERIES, BOOK 2

PATTI BENNING

SUMMER PRESCOTT BOOKS PUBLISHING

Copyright 2024 Summer Prescott Books

All Rights Reserved. No part of this publication nor any of the information herein may be quoted from, nor reproduced, in any form, including but not limited to: printing, scanning, photocopying, or any other printed, digital, or audio formats, without prior express written consent of the copyright holder.

**This book is a work of fiction. Any similarities to persons, living or dead, places of business, or situations past or present, is completely unintentional.

ONE

It was a chilly, damp autumn day, but the kitchen inside Iron and Flame was a pocket of warmth away from the dreary afternoon. Warmth, and noise. The kitchen of a busy restaurant was never quiet, and Lydia Thackery was hard-pressed to listen to her sous chef's words as she turned the beef medallion over on the griddle. It had come from a lovely, thick tenderloin, and she wanted to do the cut of meat justice. As executive chef and part-owner of the steakhouse she had opened with her ex-husband, she took pride in every single dish that left her kitchen when she was on the clock. It made for a highly stressful but satisfying career.

"So, overall, he's doing all right, but I'm not sure he's as experienced as he said he was," Chartreuse said, finishing her evaluation of Jorge Copas, their newest employee. "He's definitely newer to being a sous chef, and I think it's been slowing things down during his shifts."

"He worked at a little mom and pop place before we hired him," Lydia reminded her employee, speaking without looking at her as she prepared a plate for the tenderloin medallion. While it rested, Chartreuse would finish plating the rest of the meal. "I think it's normal that he's used to a slower pace. As long as he keeps improving and doesn't make too many easy mistakes, I'm not going to complain too much. He seems passionate about the work. At least, he did during the interview."

The younger woman nodded, her grey eyes serious. She and Lydia were both wearing matching hair nets and white aprons, though Lydia had a chef's hat to top off the ensemble.

"Yeah, he really seems to enjoy the work. I think he'll be a good fit once he gets a little more experience. I'll do another evaluation in a couple of weeks, if you want."

"Go ahead and do that," Lydia said as she carefully plated the medallion and turned off the griddle. "I'll set aside some time to work one on one with him and help him figure out what he needs to work on."

She stood there for a moment, mentally paging through her schedule. She had this weekend off, and normally she might take advantage of that to see if Jorge could come in for an extra hour or two of paid training, but she had been making an effort to focus on her life outside her job. Maybe he would be willing to come to one of his shifts an hour early next week. She made a mental note to send the request later this evening, then glanced at the clock and untied her apron.

It was four in the afternoon and the end of her shift. Jeremy wasn't here yet, but there weren't any more orders waiting for her, and she knew him well enough to know he wouldn't be more than a couple of minutes late unless it was life or death. She could say a lot of things about her ex-husband, but she wouldn't deny that he cared about Iron and Flame just as much as she did. There was a reason they had worked so hard to keep the restaurant running together even after their divorce. Life might have been easier for both of them if they had made a clean break, but easy had never been a motivator for either of them. Working out the kinks as divorced co-owners of the nicest steakhouse in town was just a different type of hard work, and they had both done plenty of heavy lifting. The fact that the restaurant was still standing was a testament to their efforts.

After saying goodbye to Chartreuse, she hung her apron and hat up, announced to the busy kitchen at large that she was leaving, then stepped through the swinging doors of the house. It was cooler out here; not enough to be chilly, but enough to be pleasant after the heat of the kitchen. Four was always an awkward time of day at the restaurant — too early for dinner, and too late for lunch — but there were still a few occupied tables. Jaelin, the lunch shift hostess, looked like she was just clocking out too, and the two servers currently on the clock were chatting near the bar while keeping an eye on their tables in case one of the customers needed something.

The bar was busier than the rest of the restaurant, though it wouldn't be packed until happy hour rolled around at five. She didn't recognize any of the patrons besides a few regulars. When she had the evening shift, she often stopped by the bar for a chat and a drink with Valerie, a regular she had started to become friends with recently, but Valerie didn't get out of work until six. For a moment, she considered seeing if her sister or another one of her friends had time to grab a drink and talk for a little while, but most of the people she knew wouldn't be out of work until later, and she wasn't sure if she would feel like going out again after she got home.

I'll do something fun this weekend, she told herself as she nodded farewell to Jaelin and left through Iron and Flame's front doors. *There's nothing wrong with having a quiet day or two.* She wrinkled her nose and glared up at the sky as a blast of wet and cold hit her face. It was sprinkling, but it was chilly enough that the tiny droplets of water felt like pinpricks of ice on her skin.

When she surveyed the parking lot for her car, she spotted a familiar figure walking toward her. Even with his shoulders hunched and the hood of his raincoat pulled up over his head, she would recognize Jeremy anywhere.

He hurried under the overhang in front of the restaurant's front door and yanked his hood back, his expression irritated. "Some day, huh? I'm sick of all this rain."

"It's better than snow," she said.

He grunted noncommittally. "How was the morning?"

"Slow. I'm almost missing the evening shift at this point." She tried to keep her tone light and joking, but judging from the tensing of his eyes, she had missed the mark.

"Look, I *told* you my therapist thought a change of pace might help. It's not forever. I'm back to taking some mornings next week, aren't I?"

"I didn't mean anything by it," she said, biting back a sigh. Running the restaurant together had gotten a little more complicated recently, after the murder of a woman Jeremy had been dating. She was trying to be understanding, she really was, but his short temper wasn't making it easy. It wasn't just with her, either; he had been shorter than usual with their employees too. He *was* getting help; she knew he was seeing a therapist and he always apologized when he snapped at someone, but she really hoped it wasn't a permanent change, because it made him a lot less pleasant to work with.

"I know." His shoulders drooped, and for a moment, he looked like he had during their divorce; tired, at the end of his rope, ready to just move on. "I'm sorry. This weather isn't helping my mood any, and I saw your sister at the grocery store this morning. She did that thing where she acts nice, but it leaves you feeling worse than ever when she's done. I heard you've been seeing her more. I'm glad, I know she's important to you."

Lillian, Lydia's sister, had never quite forgiven Jeremy for the divorce, even though Lydia had told her it was mostly mutual. The two hadn't gotten along very well, even before the divorce, so she wasn't surprised.

"I'll remind her to be nice the next time I see her," she promised.

"It's fine." He shook his head. "I'd better get in there. I don't think it'll be a busy evening, but the last few times I thought that, we ended up being slammed. See ya."

She raised her hand in farewell, then dashed through the rain to her little black SUV. As she got into the driver's seat and cranked the heat up, she glanced back at the restaurant and felt a pang at the thought of what could have been if only things had worked out between her and Jeremy.

The pang was smaller than usual, though. True, there was a life she would never have, one she had wanted for a long time, and it was hard to make peace with that, but now that she had started making a conscious effort to do more than work, sleep, and repeat, she was beginning to see that she could build a life for herself that might be even *better* than what could have been.

It might take time and effort to get there, but she was no stranger to hard work.

TWO

Lydia's home, a two-story rental on a residential street a couple of blocks away from Iron and Flame, was peaceful and quiet. It wasn't quite the comfort zone the house she used to own with Jeremy was—her landlord was strict about not painting or hanging anything that might damage the walls, so her options for decorations were lacking, and she would have given her left foot to replace the countertops in the kitchen—but it was a nice place to unwind. When the weather was nicer, she spent a lot of time in her small but private backyard, but this much cold rain kept her indoors with the heat on.

Sometimes, the house was so quiet it felt lonely, and she felt that way when she got home today. Her work schedule didn't allow for any pets other than maybe a fish, and when she looked into what it would take to get a nice tank setup, she had decided it wasn't for her. Between the water cycling, PH balances, ammonia loads, and all of the other things she would need to monitor, it seemed like it might become almost as stressful as her job.

The closest thing she had to a pet was the squirrels that liked to forage at her neighbor's birdfeeder across the street. When she got home that evening, she heated up some apple cider and settled down in her kitchen chair to warm her hands and sip her drink while she watched two of the bedraggled creatures squabble over seeds on the ground. They didn't look any happier with the rain than Jeremy was, and the comparison made her smile.

A buzz from her phone distracted her from the squirrel drama across the street, and she set her mug down to check the text message that had just come in. The sight of Jude Holloway's name brought a different sort of smile to her face, one she immediately tried to snuff out, even though there was no one else here to see it.

Jude was a game warden about her own age who she had met around the same time Audrey, Jeremy's girlfriend, passed away. He had helped her uncover the truth behind the murder and had also warned her about a man who was stalking her. She didn't know many people who would go out of their way to warn a complete stranger about something like that, and that inherent goodness in his heart was one of the reasons she had kept in touch with him even after the whole fiasco was over. Well, his warm hazel eyes didn't hurt, and neither did his cute yellow mutt named Saffron. She loved dogs, and Saffron had already managed to worm her way into her heart just a little.

She had seen Jude a handful of times since the mess surrounding Audrey's death had been straightened out and had mentioned a desire to start getting out in nature more, so she wasn't surprised to read his latest message.

It's supposed to be a nice weekend. If you're free, I'd love to show you one of my favorite trails. Let me know, and I'll tell Saffron so she can look forward to it!

Her smile crept back despite her attempts to keep it muffled. She'd had to turn down a few invitations to meet up from him due to her work schedule, which was rarely the same from week to week. Iron and Flame only had three chefs—herself, Jeremy, and an older man named Hank who was semiretired and complained something awful if they asked him to work more than twenty hours a week—which meant they were on a constant rotation that could vary wildly if one of them had something come up. She was off this weekend, though, and unless Jeremy and Hank both came down with the flu or something equally bad, her time off was almost guaranteed.

She took a moment to check the weather. Jude was right; despite the current rain and wind, it was supposed to be a nice weekend. She already had lunch plans with a friend she hadn't seen in months on Saturday, but her Sunday was open.

I would love to go for a hike Sunday morning with you and Saffron. Just let me know what time and where!

Leaning back in her chair, she started mentally sorting through her outfit options for the date. No, not a date, she mentally chided herself. She barely knew the man, and they were just friendly acquaintances for now. She didn't even know if she was ready to date again. That thought had come out of nowhere. This was just a friendly hike and something fun to do on her day off.

She might be looking forward to the weekend, but today was only Thursday, and she still had to get through the lunch shift tomorrow before she could relax. She knew better than to expect another slow day. Fridays were always busy, though they were nothing compared to the weekend. If Jeremy wanted a distraction from Audrey's death, he was doing the right thing by working all weekend.

This late in the year, it got dark early. It had still been light when she got home, but it hadn't remained that way for long. She closed the curtains, turned on the overhead lights, and puttered around the house doing laundry, surveying her fridge and making a grocery list, and finally settling down in the living room to read.

She didn't always feel lonely when she was at home by herself, but she did today, and it was making it hard for her to truly relax and unwind. The thought of calling Lillian for a chat had just crossed her mind when her phone rang. A little amused at the coincidence, she reached for it, sure that it would either be Lillian or Jude, calling to talk more about their plans for Sunday.

It was neither. The number was a local one, but unknown, and her mind flashed back to the call she had gotten in the middle of the night not long ago, alerting her of Audrey's death. But this wasn't the number to the police station—she had saved it to her phone, along with the detective's number—and there was no reason for her to worry. It was probably just a wrong number, or one of those spam calls that spoofed a local number to make her think a real person was calling.

She slid her finger across the screen to answer the call and pressed the phone to her ear.

"Hello?"

"Mom?"

The speaker was female and sounded scared and confused. Lydia blinked and shook her head, despite knowing the person on the other end of the line couldn't see her. Definitely a wrong number—she didn't have kids.

"Sorry, I think you've got the wrong number," she replied.

"Wait, don't hang up," the girl said, as if she could sense Lydia pulling the phone away from her ear. "I need help. I don't think I have time to try again. Please, can you call the police? I think he's following me, and I'm scared."

Lydia's boring, normal evening vanished in the blink of an eye. She set her book down without pausing to check the page number and sat up straighter on the edge of the couch. A sympathetic fear curled in her gut.

"Where are you? I'll call them as soon as I get off the phone with you."

"I'm—" The girl paused, and Lydia heard the sound of a car rushing by through the line. A second car followed shortly, then a third, then the traffic noise ended. She must have been by a relatively busy road. "I was waving and not one of them stopped."

"I'm sorry," Lydia said softly. Would she stop if she saw a stranger waving at her from the roadside? She liked to think she would, but it might be a different matter entirely when she was alone on a dark stretch of road after the sun had gone down. "Where are you, sweetie? I need to know where to send the police."

"I'm right by the—"

The girl broke off again, but this time there was a series of sharp sounds and rustles as if she had dropped the phone. Lydia thought she heard a scream, but the sound got cut off. The line went dead. She pulled the phone away from her face to check, and the screen showed her that the call had ended at 9:02 PM.

She stared at the blinking numbers in shocked horror for a long moment, then quickly pulled up the number pad and dialed 911. This counted as an emergency if anything did.

THREE

The police couldn't do anything. Lydia tried to understand, even as she spent the rest of the evening pacing around her living room and then tossing and turning in bed. All she could give them was the girl's phone number and the time she had called ... and the very unhelpful hint that there had been some traffic. Quarry Creek, Wisconsin was a small town, but not *that* small, and there were countless roads, streets, and highways in the radius of their area code, not to mention that the girl could have been travelling or could have moved without changing her phone number.

The dispatcher had said she would send in a request for the local police to send out an extra patrol or two, and she would put the number on file in case something came of it, and that was it. All Lydia could think about was that cut-off scream and the fear in the girl's voice. She had been trying to call her mother, for goodness' sake. She had been scared.

And Lydia hadn't been able to do a thing.

She woke up too early but knew there would be no getting back to sleep when she saw the grey dawn light streaming in around the edges of her curtains. It was seven thirty, and she didn't have to be at work for two and a half hours—three hours if she wanted to be in a rush when she got there. She checked her phone first thing, but the girl hadn't called back, and neither had the police. It was doubtful either party *would* call her, even if the issue was resolved. She didn't think they gave updates to people who called a report in, but who weren't otherwise connected to it.

She passed the time with a hot shower, even hotter coffee, and then a breakfast of a scrounged together, homemade breakfast burrito and the last slice of an apple pie she had brought home from work a week ago.

It wasn't quite the breakfast of champions, but it was filling comfort food, and that was what she needed right now.

She left for work just before ten and got there just after. Jorge, the new sous chef, had beaten her there. She suspected that Chartreuse was right, and that he wasn't quite as experienced as he had claimed, but it was clear he really wanted this job, and not just for the paycheck. He reminded her a little of herself when she was in culinary school, and once they trained him up, she thought he would be a very promising member of the team.

Noel, one of their servers, pulled in just as Lydia was getting out of her car. All three of them met by the front door; Lydia and Jorge in their more casual back of house clothes, with sneakers and as little makeup as Lydia felt like she could get away with, and Noel dressed to impress in black slacks, a maroon blouse, and sensible yet elegant black flats. Her dark blonde hair was pulled up in a short ponytail, and she had obviously spent a lot more time on her makeup than Lydia had this morning. Lydia didn't blame her—Iron and Flame was the nicest restaurant in town, and while they might not see that many four-digit guest checks, many of their customers still spent a lot and tipped well. Noel was an experienced server who knew how to get the best tips possible each day.

She might put on a bubbly personality for the guests, but with the other employees—and her bosses—she was no nonsense and to the point ... usually. Today, she seemed distracted. She barely muttered a greeting to Lydia and Jorge and walked right past them to open the door ... which was still locked. When it refused to budge, she gave the door a confused look, then blinked and turned around to see Lydia and Jorge, both watching her.

"Oh, you guys just got here too," she said. "Sorry, it's been a bad morning."

"Do you want to talk about it?" Lydia asked as she fished her keys out of her purse and stepped forward to unlock the door. "You don't need to, if it's private. Do you want me to try to get your shift covered?"

Noel shook her head. "No, it's nothing personal or anything like that. When I was driving in to work, I passed by that gas station—you know, the one with the blue roof on the state highway just north of town?" Lydia nodded, and her employee continued,

"Well, there were tons of cops parked along the road just past it. There were a few other cars in front of me, and they all slowed down to see what was going on, so I did too. I saw a white sheet covering something on the ground next to the road, and I was so distracted I almost ran into the car in front of me when they stopped. One of the cops walked over, and I thought he was going to talk to me so I rolled my window down, but he went up to the car in front of me instead, and I heard him tell the driver they couldn't stop there, and that it was the scene of an active homicide investigation." She paused to give Lydia and Jorge a wide-eyed look. "The figure on the ground was a *body*. I saw a *dead body* on my way to work today. I mean, it was covered up, but it still made me feel absolutely sick."

The keys slipped from Lydia's grasp. She heard them clatter to the ground but didn't bend to pick them up. She was too busy staring at Noel in horror. "Was the victim a woman?"

"I have no idea," Noel said. "I didn't hang around to try to find out, I can tell you that! Hey, Chef Lydia, are you all right?"

Lydia felt dizzy. Belatedly, she realized she was holding her breath, but when she tried to breathe normally, her chest felt like it was being constricted. Noel might not know whether the victim was male or female, but Lydia did; she was all but certain. She didn't have any proof, but she knew in her gut that the body Noel had seen covered in a shroud belonged to the girl who had called her the evening before.

She had called a wrong number, asked for help, and before Lydia could do anything, the call had been cut off. And now someone was dead.

"Hey, what's going on?" Noel's hands grabbed her shoulders gently, and she found herself looking into the younger woman's concerned face. "Are you all right?"

"Sorry," she said, shaking her head and trying to get herself under control. She couldn't stop wondering if she had heard the last seconds of someone's life the evening before. "We should go in."

Jorge moved to enter the restaurant, but Noel blocked the door, her arms crossed. "Uh-uh. You looked like you were having a panic attack or something. Seriously, is something wrong? Is it about what I saw on my way to work this morning?"

"It's complicated," Lydia said. "I think... I think the person who died might have called me accidentally last night. I need to figure out who it was and what happened, but it is going to have to wait. We have to get ready for opening, we have less than an hour and you know we always get a lot of takeout orders for Friday lunch."

The younger woman gave her an evaluating look, then finally relented, and the three of them went inside. Lydia went through the motions on autopilot; washing her hands, putting her apron and hat on, starting to prepare the bases for their more common dishes.

Twenty minutes after they started opening, she heard Jorge say, "Is something burning?" and realized she had been staring at an empty pot, waiting for the non-existent water inside to come to a boil. It was beginning to smoke and darken on the bottom, and she yanked it off the burner with a curse and turned the stovetop off. She set it down on a cool burner to begin shedding some of its heat and went to the sink to pour herself a glass of water, shaken. She was way too distracted today.

"You're definitely not all right," Noel said, leaning against the counter and wrinkling her nose at the lingering burnt scent. "Do you think maybe you should call off today?"

"I can't," Lydia said. "Jeremy's working this evening; he can't do an eleven-hour shift."

"What about Hank?" When Lydia continued to hesitate, Noel added, "If one of your employees knew something about a *murder*, you'd be telling us to take the day off, go to the police, and take care of ourselves. You might be my boss, and I can't make you do any of that, but you're always telling us to share our opinions and ideas, and right now my opinion is that you're not in any state to be working today."

Lydia bowed her head. Noel was right; she was too distracted and on edge to be here today.

"You've got a point. I'll call Hank and see if he's willing to pick up the morning shift today."

Assuming he was, she wanted to call the police again and see if they could tell her anything. If she just knew for sure whether the girl who had called last night and asked for help with such terror in her voice was the same person whose death the local police were investigating, she would at least be able to stop wondering. Sometimes, knowing was better than not knowing, even if the news was bad.

FOUR

The police wouldn't tell her anything. She shouldn't have been surprised, and she supposed she wasn't. She was just disappointed. The woman who answered was able to patch her through to Detective Bronner, and he listened as she explained who she was. He even took the time to look up her report from the evening before, and thanked her politely for calling to follow up, but told her he was unable to share any details of the case at this time.

And that was that. Sitting in her SUV in front of Iron and Flame, Lydia *almost* wished she hadn't taken Noel's advice and called Hank to pick up her shift. The older man had put up surprisingly little resistance to the unexpected hours, and she had only had to finish the opening routine before he arrived to take the restaurant off her hands.

There was a part of her that wished she was in there, working away on the first few orders of the day, but it was a selfish desire. She had burnt an empty pot, for goodness' sake. That was even worse than burning water—she had completely forgotten the water in the first place. She could cook under pressure; she had done some of her best work during some of the most stressful times of her life and knew that when it came down to the wire, she could focus and push through and make a nearly perfect meal in even the worst conditions.

But she wasn't stressed today. Not exactly, anyway. No, what was distracting her so much was something heavier, something that sat sourly in her gut. Guilt.

Taking a deep breath, Lydia turned the heat up a little more and then pulled up the rarely used social media app on her phone. If the police wouldn't give her the information she wanted, then maybe the internet would. She would love to prove the gut instinct that told her the victim was the girl who called her asking for help. She might feel a little silly for reacting so strongly to the news before she had any proof, but she would rather that than the alternative; that someone had needed her help and she had failed so badly they lost their life as a result.

It was easy enough to find news about the crime scene online; Quarry Creek was a growing town, but it was still small enough that there was a solid sense of community, and the locals loved to be involved in anything and everything that was happening in the area. A lot of people had seen the same thing Noel did this morning, but almost all of the posts were people asking what had happened. No one seemed to know any more than Lydia already knew; that a body had been found by the gas station on the state highway just north of town.

Then, finally, she refreshed the page and a new post popped up, written by a woman named Stephanie Wilson.

To everyone asking about the police presence near Blakley's Gas Station this morning, and to all those who have already messaged me or my family asking for details, I can confirm that my daughter, Kimberly Wilson, was found along the side of the road, deceased, in the early hours of this morning. We will not be sharing any details at this time. I ask for your understanding and compassion. Please give my family space to grieve. If you know anything about what happened, contact the Quarry Creek Police Station. We are currently working to put together a reward for any information that ends up leading to the perpetrator's arrest. You can donate at...

The post listed a website and the number to the police station. In the time Lydia had taken to read it, a few people had already left kind-hearted comments giving their condolences. There was a minor argument in the comments, where someone named Noah Robinson posted, *I can't believe she's gone. I love you, Kimberly. I'm so sorry.*

Beneath it, someone named Aiden Simmons commented, *Didn't you two break up? I hope the police take a real close look at you.*

Someone named Carter Robinson replied with, *He didn't do anything. Leave him alone.*

Aiden retorted with, *I heard them arguing all the time. It definitely wasn't a happy relationship, and women are statistically much more likely to be killed by their partner than men are.*

It continued to devolve after that, and she clicked away, feeling sick, both at the drama on a mother's post about her daughter's death, and at the confirmation that the victim was female. It still wasn't proof that it was the same girl who had called her, but the chance that she was wrong was getting smaller and smaller.

Wondering if she would get lucky and find that Kimberly had her phone number linked to her account, she looked up her social media page and took a moment to examine her profile picture. Kimberly had light brown hair, blue eyes, and a bright smile. She was twenty, according to her about page, and worked at Blakely's Gas Station. She had graduated from the Quarry Creek High School two years ago.

But despite all of that information, there was no phone number and no confirmation that her death was Lydia's fault.

She wasn't sure how long she sat in the restaurant's parking lot, scrolling through her social media app in hopes of finding more information about Kimberly's death. In the end, she admitted to herself that she wasn't going to find out the victim's phone number unless she asked someone, and reaching out to her friends or family just hours after her death was the last thing she wanted to do. The police already had her report; she would be disturbing grieving people for no reason other than her own selfish need to know.

There had to be another way to find someone's number, but unless the victim had a landline phone —and what twenty-year-old did?—she probably wasn't in the phone book. She briefly debated calling her sister, but in the end, decided that Lillian probably wouldn't have any more resources than she did. She worked at a local law firm as a paralegal, and as far as Lydia knew, that didn't give her any special privileges when it came to looking someone's number up.

She did know *one* person who might be able to help. Jude was a game warden, and that was technically law enforcement ... wasn't it? She wasn't about to ask him to do something against policy to get her that phone number, but he might have some ideas of how she could find it without skirting the law.

Instead of calling him right away, she sent him a text message, asking if he had a moment to talk. He responded more quickly than she thought he would, texting back before she had even pulled out of the parking lot, so she claimed another space to read his message.

Slow day today. You're welcome to call anytime.

She saw no reason to put it off. After dialing his number, she pressed her phone to her ear. It rang a couple of times before he answered.

"Hey, how are you doing?"

"I'm doing well," she said automatically, then winced. "Actually, no I'm not. I don't know why I said that. I was wondering, do you know how to find someone's phone number? Or get the name for a phone number you already have?"

"Should I be afraid to ask why?" he asked, sounding amused.

"It's sort of complicated. Did you hear about that woman who was found dead this morning?"

His tone sobered immediately. "I did hear about that. My coworkers and I have been talking about it all morning. It's not something you usually hear about in Quarry Creek."

"Well, I got a weird call last night, and I think it was her. I already submitted a report to the police, but it's driving me crazy not being sure, so I've been trying to figure out a way to see who the number that called me belongs to."

"Well, there are some websites that claim they'll provide you a bunch of information if you give them a phone number, but I think you have to pay, and I don't know how trustworthy they are," he said. "Have you tried looking her up online?"

"That's the first thing I did. Her number isn't linked to her account, or if it is, it's private."

"Hmm. Hold on a second. I'll be right back." The call went quiet. She heard faint noises in the background, until Jude returned. "I can take an early lunch if you want to meet up somewhere to talk. I'm guessing you aren't at work, if you're calling me."

"I ended up taking the day off," she admitted. "Are you sure? I don't want you to get into trouble."

He snorted. "Trust me, no one would care or even know if I spent all day just walking around town with Saffron and eating donuts. I just wanted to make sure my coworker would be available if any calls came in. Want to meet at the same park we did last time?"

"Sure," she said. "I'm already in town. I can swing by Morning Dove and grab some sandwiches while I wait for you, if you're hungry."

"I'm starved, and that sounds great. It'll be my treat next time."

Even though she hadn't gotten the answers she wanted yet, she was already feeling better as she said goodbye and ended the call. Having someone to talk to made all the difference in the world.

FIVE

Morning Dove was a cheerful little cafe that was kitty-corner from Iron and Flame. It was open from seven until two, and served both breakfast and lunch the entire time it was open. It was a nice place to stop at for food when she didn't want to make something during her shift at the steakhouse and knew she would be too tired to cook when she got home.

Since it was another chilly, grey day, she got both her and Jude a cup of hot coffee, then ordered a chicken salad sandwich—with dried cranberries and pecans, on a dense ancient grain bread—for her, and a hot ham and cheese sandwich for him. She knew he had ordered it before, so she figured it was a safe bet.

The park they were meeting at was a small one near the center of Quarry Creek. It had a nice, covered pavilion with picnic tables, which would be perfect for their lunch.

She beat him to the park, but only just. When she saw his work truck pull into a parking spot, she got out of her SUV with the bag of sandwiches in one hand and their coffees carried carefully with her other arm. He had his dog with him—he brought her to work sometimes—and Saffron's tail wagged the whole time she and Jude walked over to Lydia. She handed the coffee over while the dog sniffed at her shoes, then crouched down to scratch her behind the ears. She was a medium-sized mixed breed with yellow fur and mismatched ears—one pointed straight up, and the other one flopped over. It gave her a goofy appearance, one that fit well with her friendly personality.

"Have you two had a good morning so far?" she asked as she straightened up.

"It's been a pretty average day, at least if you don't count the news about the homicide," he said. "I'm glad I'm not working this weekend, though. These last couple of days have been slow because of the weather, but it's going to be a nice weekend, which means we'll have a lot of hunters out in the forest. I'm sure it'll be busy for whoever's on shift."

"Will it be safe for us to go hiking?" she asked as they walked toward the tables under the pavilion, thinking of their planned meeting on Sunday. She had never hunted herself and hadn't even considered the risks.

"Definitely," he said. "The trails I'm thinking of are busy enough that they aren't popular with hunters. We'll just wear some orange to be on the safe side—I'll bring a hat for you."

She shot him a smile in thanks as they sat down, and handed out their sandwiches while he passed her coffee over. They ate in silence for a moment before he spoke again.

"So, what exactly happened?"

Lydia put her sandwich down and took another sip of her coffee before opening her mouth and telling him all about the call last night, hearing about the murder this morning, and the little she had learned about the victim so far.

"I just know it's the same person, Jude," she said. "But I want to be sure, you know?"

"I understand," he said. "Even if it is, though, what happened isn't your fault. You know that, right?"

She shrugged, fiddling with her sandwich wrapper. "I can't think of anything else I could have done to help her, but I still feel like there should have been *something*."

"Well, let's try to figure out exactly *what* happened before you blame yourself for it too much," he said. "Do you want to swing by that gas station after this? You said she worked there, right? It might be a good place to start. The girl called you around nine? They might be able to tell us when the victim got out of work, and we can see if those times line up. And if that doesn't work, I can ask around and see if any of those websites that claim to be able to get personal information from a phone number are legit."

"I don't want you to go out of your way," she said hesitantly.

"It's my lunch break," he said with a shrug. "I need to get gas anyway. We can ride together, and I'll drop you off at your car on my way back to work. It won't take more than fifteen or twenty minutes total."

She agreed, even though she felt bad making Jude go out of his way just to try to figure out the answer to a question she was already convinced she knew the truth to. They finished their sandwiches—she really liked Morning Dove's chicken salad, but she wished she had gotten something warm to help offset the chilly day—then took a quick walk around the park with Saffron, who took great joy in finding sticks for Lydia to admire.

Back at Jude's truck, he opened the passenger side door and leaned the seat forward so Saffron could hop onto the small bench in the back of the cab, then returned the seat to its proper position so she could get in. His work truck smelled like cloves, for some reason, and had a few questionable stains on the upholstery, and the door creaked alarmingly when she pulled it shut, but when he turned the engine on, the heat blasted out even more powerfully than the heat in her considerably newer SUV.

"Sorry," he said, his voice raised over the sound of the heater. "The fan only works on the highest setting. These trucks are ancient, and we don't get enough funding to replace them as often as we should. We can either have high heat or no heat, your choice."

"Let's keep the heat on, I can always roll down the window if it gets too warm," she said, holding her hands up in front of the vent to defrost her fingers. She hadn't brought much in the way of winter gear with her, since she had been expecting to spend all day in a warm kitchen.

With Saffron's panting head between them, Jude put the truck into gear and drove out of town, toward the gas station. Lydia kept her eyes peeled as they drove down the state highway north of town. She didn't know exactly where Noel had seen the body, only that it was somewhere between the gas station and Quarry Creek. When she did finally spot the right area, it was only because she had been looking so closely; the only sign that anything happened was a section of torn up, muddy grass along the west side of the road where the emergency vehicles had pulled off the road.

Jude slowed as they passed it, but didn't say anything, his expression somber.

STEAKING A CLAIM

Blakely's Gas Station was run down and rickety looking, with only two pumps, a tiny parking area, and a convenience store inside that was absolutely packed with junk food, energy drinks, and over-priced novelty items. Lydia had been there plenty of times throughout her life, though she preferred the newer and cleaner gas station on the other side of town. She didn't come here often enough to recognize any of the employees on sight, and as Jude parked by one of the pumps, cracked the windows for Saffron, and they got out of the car, she wondered if she had spoken to Kimberly before without even knowing it.

"Looks like they're open," Jude murmured as they approached the door. "I'm a little surprised they didn't close for the day if one of their employees was killed."

"Me too," Lydia said. "But by the looks of the place, they might not be able to afford to lose the business."

The paint was peeling on the sides of the building, and one of the windows was cracked. An old security camera looked down at them from above the door, and when she entered the building, she saw another one above the register, along with a faded sign that read *Smile, you're on camera!*

Maybe the security footage would help the police figure out what happened. The scene where the body was found was only about a quarter of a mile down the road, maybe less. Though why Kimberly would have been walking out there, Lydia didn't know. It was about two miles into town, which was too far for most people to want to walk on a cold, rainy night like last night.

"Bathroom's for paying customers only, if that's what you're looking for."

The man who spoke was half-hidden behind a shelf lined with bags of chips, a mop in his hand that he was half-heartedly swiping at the floor with. He had a displeased, unfriendly expression on his face, and watched them with narrowed eyes. His grey t-shirt was stained, and his thin greying hair looked unbrushed.

"We're here to get gas," Jude said. He glanced at Lydia. "Do you want anything else? I might get a pop for the road."

"I'm fine," she said. "Thanks."

"Well, watch out, I just mopped that part of the floor," the older man said. "Don't want you fallin' and tryin' to sue or anything, so don't say I didn't warn ya."

"I'll watch my step. Thanks for the warning," Jude said. He moved away toward the refrigerated section to find his drink, leaving Lydia to wander over toward the register. The older man put the mop down and walked around the counter, sitting down with a grunt on the stool behind it. She noticed he was wearing a faded nametag that read *Brandon* on his shirt.

"How much you want, and what pump are you at?" he asked, wiggling the mouse to wake up the computer.

"Oh, he's paying," she said, turning to nod at Jude. "I was actually wondering if you could answer a question for me."

"Won't know 'till you ask."

"Right." She took her phone out of her purse and brought up the number that had called her the night before. "Can you tell me if this number belongs to one of your employees, Kimberly Wilson?"

She had been expecting a reaction when she said the girl's name and wasn't surprised when his eyes narrowed again, and he crossed his arms. "You a reporter or somethin'? I don't want none of that. What happened to her was bad enough, don't need more trouble."

"No, nothing like that," she said. "She called me, you see. Or someone called me. I think it was her, and I think I might have heard her get attacked, but I don't have any way to confirm that it was her number, and I don't want to bother her family about it right now."

He frowned and gave her a measuring, suspicious look for a few breathless seconds before finally grunting and pulling open a drawer, where he removed an old notebook. He flipped through it, ran a finger down the page, then turned it around to show her.

Kimberly's name was written in a messy scrawl, and next to it, was the phone number that was currently pulled up on the screen of Lydia's phone.

SIX

"So, you know what happened to her, do you?" he asked as he pulled the notebook back.

Still reeling with the confirmation that what she suspected was true—the girl who called her begging for help was the same young woman who had been murdered the night before—she shook her head slowly.

"No. I don't know more than anyone else. All I know is that she was scared, and she knew someone was after her. Was she working here yesterday evening?"

Brandon nodded. "That she was. She was supposed to get out at nine, but I let her go a few minutes early because she was getting worried about walking home so late. Always asking to leave early or showing up late, that one."

"She was walking home? There's nothing out here. Did she live along the highway somewhere?"

There were a handful of secluded, rural houses along the highway into town. Most of them were set far enough back from the road that they weren't visible to anyone driving by, and the handful Lydia had seen in the course of visiting friends or attending garage sales had been larger and fancier than anything in town. She suspected that anyone who lived in one of those houses probably wasn't working at a gas station with no car.

"You know that apartment complex right on the edge of town to your right, when you're driving south down the road? She lived there," Brandon told her. "Think it's two or three miles from here. One of her neighbors used to drive her, but he stopped out of the blue a couple weeks ago, and she's been walking ever since. Don't know why he stopped and didn't care to ask. As long as she kept showing up for her shifts, I figured it wasn't any of my business."

Lydia felt a surge of sympathy for Kimberly. She knew she was unsafe but hadn't been able to do anything about it. She had needed this job badly enough to walk miles each day, even as the weather grew steadily more chilly. She hated that she had been unable to help the girl. It was going to eat at her for a long, long time to come.

She heard Jude approaching and moved over to give him room. He set a bottle of pop down by the register and took out his wallet while Brandon rang it up. After telling him how much gas he wanted, he glanced at the security camera above the counter.

"I couldn't help but overhear what the two of you were talking about," he said. "Do you know if your cameras caught anything?"

Brandon ran his card and handed it back, shaking his head with a scoff. "These old things? They don't work worth nothing. This one over the register doesn't work at all, and the one out front only works if you jiggle it just so and then don't so much as let a butterfly breathe on it. The wires must be bad. I just keep them up to make any troublemakers think twice. Told the police the same thing, but of course they want to go digging through the old computer that's hooked up to the cameras. I told him they can either get a warrant or forget about it. They're not going to find anything on there anyway, and I won't have them invading my privacy for nothing."

"Well, if your cameras didn't catch anything, did you *see* anything? Do you have any idea who did it?" Lydia asked. "You were here last night, right?"

"I'll tell you the same thing I told the police," he said. "The only person I can think of is that boyfriend of hers. Her ex now, I guess. They broke up a couple weeks ago. Around the same time her neighbor stopped driving her to work, now that I think about it. Good riddance if you ask me. Before they broke up, he and his brother were always in here, chatting with her and distracting her from her job. I've barely seen him since, but his brother was in here last night, so he might have been waiting out in the car for all I know. He left a while before her shift ended, though."

"Why do you think her ex might have had something to do with it?" Lydia asked. "Did they fight a lot?"

"Not that I know of, but it doesn't take much to make a brash young man lash out when a pretty girl spurns him, you know? And my gut tells me it was someone she knew. Sure, we get outsiders coming through Quarry Creek plenty these days, but it was a quiet night, and it seemed to me like she was extra jumpy before she left. Like she knew there was someone out there waiting for her."

He lowered his voice a tad, like he was telling a scary story, not recounting his employee's last night alive. Fighting back a shudder, Lydia thanked him while Jude accepted his receipt, and they took their leave.

She had learned what she hoped to learn, but confirming that Kimberly was the same girl who called her in a panic the night before only made her more determined to figure out what happened to her. She hadn't been able to prevent the girl's death, but maybe she could help her get the justice she deserved after the fact.

SEVEN

Lydia had called Jude with the vague hope that he would be able to make her feel better. That hadn't happened, though she was still grateful to him for spending his lunch break with her and going to the gas station so she could confirm what she already knew.

As they drove back to the park in town, she knew he could tell that her mood hadn't improved—if anything it was even worse, because now she was absolutely certain Kimberly died because she, Lydia, hadn't done enough to help her. Still, she assured him she was going to be fine, thanked him again for eating lunch with her, promised she would see him

Sunday, then reached into the back to pat Saffron goodbye and got out of the truck.

He looked concerned and skeptical as he slowly put his truck into gear and reversed out of the parking spot, but he left all the same, and as soon as he was out of sight, she let her expression crumple.

A young woman, a girl only twenty years old, had called her in a desperate plea for help, and she had died because Lydia hadn't done enough.

It was a good thing Noel had convinced her to take the day off, because she had no idea how she would have managed to function at the restaurant in the state she was in.

She drove straight home and, lacking anything better to do, dove into cleaning the kitchen with ferocity. She emptied out the fridge, scrubbed all the shelves, reorganized the freezer and the pantry, ran her oven's self-cleaning cycle, and even looked up how to clean the filter in the dishwasher, something she'd had on her mental to-do list for a long time.

Cleaning didn't make her feel better, but at least it gave her something to do with her hands while her mind was preoccupied. She ended up getting a lot of housework done that day, and spent the last part of the evening online, scouring local social media for updates about Kimberly's case.

There weren't any, but there was an outpouring of compassion toward her family. As much as her heart ached for them, she refrained from typing out a message of her own. She didn't think it would be right, not when she was partially responsible for Kimberly's death.

Saturday dawned clear, except for a few puffy white clouds high in the sky, and slightly warmer than Friday had been. It was a perfectly cheery sort of day, and it didn't match Lydia's mood at all. She was sorely tempted to cancel her lunch with Taylor. The only thing keeping her from doing it was a sense of shame—she had all but ghosted her friends after the divorce, and she really didn't want to repeat the same mistake now that she was beginning to reach out to them again. She decided to go to lunch as planned, instead of moping around her house alone. Maybe talking about what was bothering her would help. Maybe it wouldn't, but she knew for a fact that staying here alone wouldn't make her feel any better.

Before she sank so far into the life of a hermit that she had almost forgotten what it was like to maintain a healthy social life, meeting friends for a meal at Iron and Flame had been a normal occurrence. As owner—or co-owner—her meals were written off, and she also knew what was in season, what the specialties of the chef on shift were, and they were guaranteed to get the best service when they ate there. She didn't eat at Iron and Flame as a guest nearly as often as Jeremy did—she preferred to make her meals herself and take them home to eat when she was done with her shift—but when she did, she always made sure to tip well. The meals themselves might be free, but her employees' labor wasn't.

Sometimes she felt as if Jeremy took advantage of this system when he took his many, many dates here to eat for free. The arrangement had worked better when they were still married and only occasionally went out with friends. She knew it wasn't something he would be interested in changing, though, and it was a battle she had decided not to pick.

When she arrived at Iron and Flame that morning, half an hour after opening, she felt a little out of place. She almost never stopped in when she wasn't here to work or do something related to work, and it was just plain weird to be seated and given a menu just like anyone else.

The hostess winked at her and made an obvious show of pretending not to know who she was as she gave her normal spiel about their weekly specials and seasonal vegetables. Playing along cheered Lydia up a little, and to her surprise, seeing Taylor come through the doors and wave to her across the restaurant before approaching boosted her mood even more.

Kimberly's death still sat heavy on her heart, but getting out for lunch and seeing her friend was a good reminder that there was much more to the world than the little box she tended to live in.

"Oh, my goodness, Lydia. How long has it been?" Taylor said as she sat down. "Your hair is gorgeous, as always. I think it's even longer than it was last time I saw you."

"Thanks," Lydia said, raising a hand to touch her red hair self-consciously. It had always been one of her favorite features about herself. Back when she and Jeremy were together, they had made a striking couple, with his dark, nearly black hair and her own deep red hair. It was where the name of the restaurant came from—Iron and Flame, Jeremy and Lydia. They were a power couple, once. Now, she wasn't sure if her old self would even recognize the person she was today. "You look great. Are you still running?"

"Oh, yeah," Taylor said with a laugh. "I have another marathon scheduled for this coming spring. It's supposed to be motivation for me to get out and exercise during the winter, but I'm already dreading those cold days. How are you? Are you seeing anyone new? Are things still going all right with Jeremy?"

She wrinkled her nose and glanced around the restaurant as she said his name, as if expecting him to pop out from behind a table. Lydia knew he was on shift in the kitchen right now, but it was unlikely that they would see him. He had no reason to pop out and talk to her, and Saturdays were busy enough that he probably wouldn't have time anyway.

"Things with Jeremy are the same as ever," Lydia said. "I'm not dating anyone, but—"

She broke off mid-sentence. She'd been about to mention Jude, but it felt too early to do that. She had seen him a handful of times, and sure, they were planning on going for a hike tomorrow, but she wasn't sure if either of them wanted anything more than friendship.

"You can't leave me hanging," Taylor said. "But? Who's the special someone?"

She sighed. "I met this guy. Jude Holloway. He's a game warden, and really into outdoorsy stuff—you'd probably like him, actually. He has a dog. We aren't dating or anything like that, but we've been spending time together. I'm not sure if I'm ready to start dating yet, but he's the first person I've felt like I might be interested in since the divorce."

"Lydia, girl, it's been years. You need to get back out there. Go on a date with this Jude guy—ask him if he doesn't ask you first—and have some fun. You don't have to marry the first guy you date, but you can't be alone forever."

"I'll see where things go," Lydia hedged. "How about you? How's Martin?"

Lydia listened with half an ear as Taylor talked about her husband. Everything her friend had said about her dating life, she had heard before. Her friends had tried desperately to get her back into the dating game almost as soon as her and Jeremy's divorce was finalized, but she was surprised to find that she was actually considering it now.

She wanted to get married again at some point. She knew that much. She missed having a partner, someone who would always be there for her and vice versa. She wanted that for herself, she just hoped she wasn't too late to find it. She was in her thirties now, and while that was far from decrepit, she knew her clock was ticking. There were only so many good men in the world, and if she wanted to find someone better than Jeremy, she had her work cut out for her.

"Enough about my life," Taylor said when she was done catching Lydia up on the past few months. "I want to hear more about you. You just disappeared on us. We've all been worried about you. Are you doing better now?"

"I was quite the workaholic for a while," Lydia admitted. "I'm making more of an effort now, though. A few things happened to make me realize that if I want my life to change, I'm going to have to make the effort to change it myself. I know I've been a terrible friend for a while, but I'm going to try to make up for it."

"You know you're welcome to rejoin our brunches anytime you want," Taylor said. "We'd all be happy to have you back. You look tired, though. Did you work late yesterday?"

"No," Lydia admitted. "It's kind of a long story, and it's not a happy one."

"Well, we've got all afternoon. Let's order, then you can tell me what happened."

They put their orders in—Lydia opted for a winter squash soup and a chicken salad with house dressing, while Taylor got a burger and fries with their secret sauce. She spent a few moments asking Lydia what the secret recipe was before she got down to business.

"All right, spill. What happened?"

Lydia took a deep breath, then proceeded to tell Taylor all about the call, hearing about Kimberly's death, and her conversation with the young woman's boss at the gas station.

"And before you say anything, I know that, realistically, I did everything I could," she said when she was finished. "That's what my mind says, at least. But in my heart, I can't help but feel like I failed her. She was twenty, Taylor. Do you remember being twenty? We had our whole lives ahead of us. That poor girl, she's never going to get to live the life she should have had. She asked me for help, and I couldn't help her."

"Oh, Lydia," Taylor said sadly. "You can't blame yourself for that. I heard what happened—I had no idea you were connected to it, though—and my heart breaks for her and her family too. Things like that shouldn't happen here in Quarry Creek. A friend of mine lives in the same apartment building Kimberly did, and she called me last night to talk about it. She's feeling pretty terrible about it too. Kimberly didn't deserve what happened to her, but you don't deserve to feel guilty for something that wasn't your fault."

Lydia took in her friend's words, but her mind focused on one thing. "Hold on, you know someone who lives in the same building Kimberly did?"

"Yeah, I met her at the gym. She's a little younger than us, around twenty-five, I think. She lives a couple doors down from where Kimberly lived."

"Would you mind giving her my number? I know it probably seems crazy, but I really want to know more about Kimberly and what happened to her. I can't help but feel connected to her somehow, even though I only spoke to her for a minute or two and she never even knew my name."

"Of course. I'll pass on your number, and I'll tell her a little bit about why you want to talk to her. For the record, I don't think it's crazy. Sometimes the universe just connects two people, and you don't realize why until later."

Lydia felt a lump in her throat as she gave her friend a grateful smile. Why had she ever stopped seeing Taylor and the rest of her friend group? Sure, keeping up with her friends made her life busy sometimes, and it could be difficult to put in the emotional labor and the time it took to be a good friend, but it was worth it. She was determined not to let her world get so small again.

EIGHT

After lunch, Lydia went home. She kept her phone's volume turned up in case Taylor's friend called her, but she didn't get any calls or text messages all evening. She tried not to be impatient—she didn't know if Taylor had even reached out to her friend yet, and it was very likely the other woman wouldn't be interested in talking to a stranger about her neighbor who had recently passed away. It was a big thing to ask of someone she didn't even know.

When the waiting got to be too much for her, she got back online and read the few updates on Kimberly's murder that she could find. The police still hadn't announced any arrests, and her family had posted a reward of a couple thousand dollars for any information leading to a suspect. She clicked on the post to read the comments, and spotted Noah Robinson's name again. This time, his comment read, *I will chip in $500 as well. We all want to know what happened.*

Under it was a comment from Carter Robinson that read, *Another $500 from me. #JusticeForKimberly.*

Hadn't one of them claimed to be dating Kimberly in the other post? She thought so, but wasn't certain, so she clicked on Carter's profile and scrolled to his friend list. There, she found Kimberly's name. There was no relationship status, but if they had broken up, there wouldn't be one. They had been friends for six years, according to his friend list. Just teenagers when they first met each other. She scrolled up to find Noah's name under the family section of the friend list and clicked on it. He was in his mid-twenties, with a roman nose and curly brown hair. He looked nice. *Earnest.* She tried to imagine him killing someone and couldn't. A little digging showed her he had been friends with Kimberly for only five years.

Was Carter or Noah the one who had been dating her? A little confused, but certain one of these men was the ex Brandon had mentioned, she returned to

Kimberly's profile and scrolled down past all of the recent public posts, her fingers crossed that when Kimberly changed her relationship status, it had updated her feed.

Sure enough, after a lot of scrolling, there it was. Three weeks ago, she had gone from *In a Relationship With Noah Robinson* to *Single*. She must have been close to both brothers, Lydia thought. According to Brandon, her ex's brother—so, Carter—had been in the gas station the day she died, though he had left before she got off her shift. Was it a coincidence, or had one or both brothers had something to do with her death?

She clicked back to the original post about the reward, but she didn't see any other comments that jumped out at her. Sighing, she exited out of the web browser and decided to start meal prepping for the week. She was too on edge to relax in front of the TV, and at least with cooking, she could get something productive done while keeping her mind busy.

By the time she finished meal prepping her breakfast burritos and chicken chili for the week, it was dark out. She could call it an early night, but she wasn't tired and knew she would just lay in bed, tossing and turning. She could call Lillian to chat, but she knew her sister would be worried if she knew Lydia was getting involved in this homicide case, even if all she was doing was looking things up online and asking questions.

After some deliberation, she decided to drive up to the murder scene and gas station again. She wanted to see exactly how far the walk from the gas station to the apartment complex was. It didn't feel that bad in the car, but on foot it would be a long, dark walk along a road that didn't have a sidewalk and barely even had a shoulder for someone to walk on.

It wasn't a walk she would want to do in the dark, and it was hard to imagine Kimberly doing it twice a day every day to get to and from work.

Leaving the lights on to greet her when she came back, Lydia went outside, got into her SUV, and pulled out of her driveway. During the day, Quarry Creek was a little quaint, but warm and welcoming. She liked the town and had always felt at home there. At night, and especially so soon after a murder took place, the town had a different feel. The dark forest that surrounded the town felt ominous. When she reached the apartment complex on the edge of town, she slowed, reset her trip counter, and kept an eye on it as she headed toward the gas station. She kept her speed lower than the posted limit out of fear of hitting deer, and only had one car pass her on the road. It wasn't very busy, which meant it would be a very lonely trip for someone who was walking in the dark.

She was surprised to find a car pulled off the road right next to the muddy tracks where the emergency vehicles had been parked after Kimberly's body was discovered. Its hazards were on, and the passenger side door was open. At first, she wondered if someone had been in an accident, and she slowed down even further.

There were two people on the side of the road near the car. One was walking back and forth along the shoulder a little north of the car, closer to the gas station. The other was further off the road and seemed to be using his phone's flashlight to look for something in the tall grass.

The second figure was the one who turned toward her as her car approached and jogged over to the edge of the road, waving his flashlight in a signal for her to pull over. She hesitated but knew how deeply she regretted not being able to help Kimberly more, and decided to see what they wanted in case there was something she could do for them.

She pulled over to the right side of the road and put her hazards on. The figure that had waved her down paused briefly to look for cars before he jogged across the road toward her. She rolled her window down, but only a couple of inches.

She wanted to help if she could, but she didn't want to end up like Kimberly.

"How can I help you?" she asked when the stranger was a couple of feet away, raising her voice slightly so her words would cover the distance.

She still couldn't see much past the light of his phone. He raised it to shine the light through the window at her, and she held up a hand to shield her eyes.

"Sorry," he said, lowering the phone and shutting the flashlight off.

It took her eyes a moment to adjust to the sudden darkness, but when they did, the light from her headlights was enough for her to make out his facial features. For all that he was a stranger, he was surprisingly familiar; a man with curly brown hair and a roman nose who looked like he was in his mid-twenties.

"Do you need something?" she asked. Her tone was a little sharper than she intended, but this whole situation had her on edge.

"I was hoping we could ask you some questions. Are you a local? Hold on—Carter, come over here!"

He turned to wave to his companion. When she heard the name, her mind made the connection immediately. She knew why this man looked so familiar. She had seen his face on her laptop's screen not even an hour ago.

He was Noah Robinson, Kimberly's ex, and though she hadn't gotten a look at the other man's face yet, she was willing to bet he was here with his brother. Her guess was confirmed when Carter jogged across the road and walked through the light from her headlights to join them.

"What's going on?" he asked.

He had the same nose as his brother, but his hair was lighter and straighter, and he had a set of military dog tags around his neck. They looked old—

probably a relative's instead of his own. Noah was a little taller than him, but despite the small differences, it was obvious they were related.

"We aren't finding anything looking around in the dark like we were. I think we need to start talking to people." He gestured at Lydia before refocusing his gaze on her. She realized he was still waiting for an answer.

"I am a local," she said. "How can I help you?"

"Do you drive this road a lot in the evenings?" Noah asked. "If you drive by this spot at the same time every day, you may have seen my girlfriend, Kimberly, walking to and from the gas station she works at."

"Ex-girlfriend," Carter chimed in.

Lydia glanced at the clock and realized it was just past nine. Purely by coincidence, she had come out here at almost the exact same time Kimberly was attacked. The thought raised goosebumps on her skin.

"I don't normally drive this route, no," she said instead of explaining all of that. "I've never seen her."

"Well, did you hear about the murder?" Noah asked. "That was her. She was killed on Thursday night. Are you sure you didn't see anything?"

"Not even a car, or someone walking down the road?" Carter added. "Did you stop at Blakely's Gas Station at all on Thursday?"

"No to all of that," Lydia said. A part of her wondered if she should tell them about the phone call, but it was dark, these men were strangers, and Noah was very likely to be a prime suspect in her death. "I hardly ever take this road. I just couldn't sleep tonight and decided to go for a drive. Sorry I couldn't help."

She put her car into drive and turned off her hazards, a clear sign she was ready to leave. To her relief, both of them stepped back to give her the space to pull away from the shoulder. She rolled her window all the way up as she set the car into motion, and started mentally mapping out her route home so she wouldn't have to drive past them again.

She couldn't blame them for trying to figure out what happened to Kimberly, but as much as she wanted to know the truth herself, she had to remember that the killer was still out there somewhere. For the first time, it occurred to her that Kimberly's call to her might have painted a target on her back. If the killer learned someone had witnessed Kimberly's last moments, even if just over the phone, what would they do?

NINE

It seemed like no matter what she did, she couldn't escape from Kimberly's death. She got terrible sleep that night and woke up cranky and groggy. Still, she forced herself to get ready for the hike with Jude and Saffron. She didn't want to cancel on him and was looking forward to seeing him more than she wanted to admit.

She was about to leave to meet him at the trailhead when her phone buzzed. She paused to check it, in case he was texting to let her know he was going to be late. The text wasn't from him, though. It was from a local, unknown number.

Hey, is this Lydia? This is Terri, Taylor's friend. You asked her to pass your number on to me to talk about

Kimberly. I'm free all day, so stop by anytime. I'm in apartment 2B. Just shoot me a text a few minutes before you get here.

Taylor had come through for her after all. Lydia locked up the house and sat in her SUV while she responded, doing some quick mental math to figure out when she would be able to meet Terri. Mid-afternoon was probably the earliest she could commit to—she wasn't sure how long the hike with Jude would take, and she didn't want to rush it, no matter how desperately she wanted to know more about Kimberly and the reason behind her death.

After sending the text, she pulled out of her driveway and tried not to think about the coming meeting too much. The afternoon would get here at its own pace, and she didn't want to be distracted for the entire hike.

The trailhead Jude had picked out was a lot more intensive than walking around the local park. Lydia couldn't think about much other than navigating the trail and taking her next step. It made her realize how out of shape she was, though at least she managed to keep up with Jude without holding him back too much.

Saffron barely seemed to notice the elevation gain. The yellow dog bounded ahead of them on a long leash, pausing every once in a while to wait for them, her brown eyes seeming to urge them to hurry up. They stopped for a break when they reached the top of the large hill and took in the view, then finished the loop that led them back to the parking lot. By the time they reached their vehicles, Lydia was sweaty and sore, but she had to admit it was fun.

"I don't go on very many adventures these days," she said as they unlocked their cars. "I can see why you like that trail. The hills are terrible, but when you get to the top, the view is beautiful. We could see the whole town."

"I like that it's a loop, too," Jude said. "It's never as much fun to backtrack over ground you've already covered. I'm glad you enjoyed it. Do you want to go get coffee or lunch together now?"

"I would love to, but I already have another commitment," she said.

She wondered if she should tell him she was going to talk to someone about Kimberly, but she had a feeling he would think it was odd that she was getting so involved in all of this. He had already been kind enough to go to the gas station with her on Friday. She didn't want him to think she was completely batty.

"Some other time then," he said with a smile. "I had a nice time today, Lydia. Thank you for joining me."

She thanked him for inviting her, crouched down to give Saffron a goodbye scratch behind the ears, then got into her SUV and hurried home. She had been hoping to go straight to the apartment complex to talk with Terri, but she desperately needed to shower and change first.

She got to the apartment complex later than she expected, but Terri told her to come on up when she texted that she was there. She grabbed her purse and locked her car, then entered the apartment building, pausing just once to look around. It was odd to think Kimberly had lived here, a woman she had never met, yet felt so connected to after one wrong number call on a fateful night.

She made her way up the stairs and found apartment 2B. Terri opened the door before she could knock and gestured her in.

"Take your shoes off and make yourself at home," she said. "I'm curious. Taylor said you never met Kimberly, but she called you the night she was killed? How does that work?"

Lydia slipped off her shoes and glanced around the apartment. It was clean and modern feeling, with a plush rug and a potted plant that was nearly as tall as the ceiling by the window.

"I think she was trying to call her mom," Lydia said. "She must have been in a hurry and dialed a wrong digit. She told me someone was following her—she said 'he,' so I'm pretty sure whoever attacked her was male. It all happened so fast. I called the police when the call got cut off, but there wasn't much they could do because she hadn't been able to tell me where she was."

"Oh, wow, I can't even imagine," Terri said. "No wonder you're so curious about her. I didn't know Kimberly super well—we were on friendly terms, but I wouldn't say we were actually *friends*, so I'm not sure how much I'll be able to help you. What exactly did you want to know?"

"Well, I talked to her boss at the gas station… Brandon, I think his name was?" Terri nodded when she paused, and she continued, "He mentioned a neighbor used to drive her to and from work. Was that you?"

Terri shook her head. "No, that was Aiden. He's in the apartment between mine and hers. I know they used to be close, but I think they had some sort of falling out. I'm not sure why. All I know is she started asking me to bring her mail in when she went to visit her mom, instead of asking him. He's a nice guy, so I have no idea what went wrong. He works from home, actually. He's probably in right now. Do you want to talk to him?"

"I'm not sure, it might be kind of strange coming out of the blue like this—"

"Hey, I'm curious too. We might not have been super close, but she was still someone I knew, you know? I want to know what happened to her as much as anyone does. If she had something else going on in her life, Aiden is more likely to know than me. Here, grab your shoes, and we'll go next door."

Lydia was still stuffing her shoes onto her feet in the hallway when Terri raised her fist and knocked on Aiden's door. It only took a few moments for him to open it. Aiden looked like he was in his thirties,

Lydia's age or maybe a little older. He was wearing rectangular glasses and had a plaid bathrobe thrown on over a pair of worn jeans.

"What is it, Terri?" he asked, irritated. "I've got a video call in about five minutes, and I still have to put actual clothes on."

"This is Lydia. She was on the phone with Kimberly when she was attacked, which means she probably heard the last few minutes of her life. She's trying to figure out what happened, and we were both wondering if you knew if someone else was giving her rides, since you stopped. Why did you stop, anyway? She had to walk all the way home from the gas station, you know. It's only a couple minutes' drive, but it's a least a forty-minute walk."

Terri spoke rapid fire, like she had to get all the words out before someone interrupted her.

"Are you trying to blame me for what happened?" Aiden asked. "*She* asked *me* to stop offering her rides. I didn't just quit driving her out of the blue. And no, I don't think anyone else was giving her rides either."

"Not even Noah?" Terri asked. "I always wondered why she was walking back and forth to work instead of asking him."

"They broke up," Aiden said shortly.

Lydia had already known that, but it seemed Terri didn't, because she gasped. "She broke up with Noah? What happened?"

Aiden sighed, running a hand across his face. He looked tired and annoyed. "It was my fault, I guess. They got into an argument a couple weeks ago. He was shouting at her, and she was just giving these quiet one-word responses. It wasn't the first time, either. I don't think he treated her very well, and I just had enough of it that night. I ended up calling the police about a domestic disturbance. They didn't do much other than ask them to keep it down. After the police left, Noah came over to my apartment and told me to stay out of their business. I told him I'd only butt out if Kimberly asked me to. She was standing right there, and he turned around and waited for her to defend him, I guess, but she didn't say anything. He got quiet, but I could tell he was upset. They went back into her apartment, and I couldn't hear any more arguing, but when I knocked on her door to see if she needed a ride to work the next morning, she told me Noah broke up with her because she was bad at setting boundaries with other people, and that she didn't want me to give her rides anymore. She was upset, and I felt like a jerk. We didn't talk much after that."

"Hold on, you're saying Noah broke up with her?" Lydia said.

"That's what she said."

She realized she had been assuming Kimberly was the one to break their relationship off. If Noah was the one who ended their relationship, then feeling spurned wouldn't have been a motive for him to kill her, like Brandon had suggested it might be.

"Well, I've got to go," Aiden said. "My video call is in roughly two minutes now. Don't forget, Terri, they're doing inspections next month. If you want to hide your cat in my apartment again, you need to tell me a couple days in advance. Don't just show up at eight in the morning with a cat and a litter box again."

"Yeah, yeah," Terri said. "Thanks, Aiden. See you around."

He shut the door and they returned to Terri's apartment. This time, Lydia stood just inside the door so she wouldn't have to take her shoes off and put them back on again.

"I didn't know she and Noah broke up," Terri said. "That's just crazy. They were together for a long time. I think she went to high school with him and his brother, and they were always super close. They were over here almost every day, and I swear I've still been seeing their car in the parking lot. I would have noticed if it suddenly stopped showing up."

"You saw their car in the parking lot?" Lydia asked. "Do the Robinson brothers share a vehicle?"

"Yeah, as far as I know. I think they're renting a house together somewhere in town. I remember Kimberly complained about it, because she wanted to move in with Noah next year, but she didn't want Carter living with them. But yeah, I've definitely seen their car around. Maybe they got back together, and she just didn't tell Aiden."

"Maybe," Lydia said. *Or maybe her ex was stalking her*, she thought. "Well, thanks for talking to me. I'm not sure what to think about all of this, but at least it clears some things up."

"No problem, I'm glad I could help. Let me know if you figure anything out."

Lydia promised she would. She raised her hand in farewell and set off down the stairs. She was exhausted from the hike and had reached a dead end in investigating Kimberly's death and was looking forward to taking the rest of the day off before going back to work tomorrow.

TEN

She had the evening shift on Monday, which meant she got there at four and said a brief hello to Jeremy in passing as he left. It felt good to get back to work, even if she was a little self-conscious, considering that last time she saw Noel, she had been on the verge of a panic attack, and her employee had been forced to convince her to take the day off. Noel didn't mention anything about it though, just gave her a kind smile before making a sandwich to eat during her break.

—Chartreuse was working today—Jorge had most of the weekend shifts with Jeremy, and she still had to find out how that had gone; she had completely forgotten to set aside more training time for him—

and they settled into a comfortable routine in the kitchen.

It was a busy day, but Lydia was able to take a short break just after eight, and spent it at the bar, drinking a cold glass of water to rehydrate while she picked at a seared tuna appetizer. She never ate much during her shift, since heavy meals slowed her down, but she had to eat something to keep her energy up.

"Hey, stranger," a familiar voice said.

She turned to see Valerie slide onto the stool next to her. Valerie had gotten caught up in an MLM scheme a couple of months ago, and Lydia had first met her when she was trying to sell some essential oils. She had reached out to Lillian to see if her sister had any advice, and after Valerie managed to get out of the hole she had dug herself into, she and Lydia had kept in touch. Valerie came into the restaurant a few times each week to grab a drink and a takeout meal, and Lydia usually took a few minutes to chat with her if she was on shift and had the time.

"Hey, yourself. How was your weekend?"

"It was nowhere near long enough. I'm looking forward to the holidays. I get a week off for Christmas, and I'm going to spend the entire time in my PJs. Do you have to work over the holidays?"

"Well, we're closed on Christmas itself, and we're only open for takeout on Christmas Eve," Lydia said. "I'm not sure whether Jeremy or I will be working on Christmas Eve, but either way, it's fine. So, no, I don't get much time off, but I'm used to it."

"Oof, I don't envy you," Valerie said. "Are you on break right now?"

"Yeah, but I should—" She broke off as her cell phone buzzed. Valerie rose to her feet, seeming to sense her distraction.

"Go ahead and answer it," she said. "I'm just here to pick up an order, anyway. Call me later and we can chat, all right?"

As one of the servers handed Valerie her to-go bag, Lydia nodded. She waved farewell as her friend left, then tapped her phone's screen to wake it up so she could check her notifications. The text message was from her sister.

I've got to get my tires rotated tomorrow morning. Want to meet for breakfast while I wait for the shop to get done with it?

She smiled as she responded in the affirmative. Lillian was her closest family member, both in terms of relationship and physically, since she lived in Quarry Creek. Their parents had moved away years ago, after their daughters moved away for college and before they had moved back for their careers. She had been making an effort to spend more time with her sister lately, and they had been meeting once or twice a week for a while now.

She knew she should get back to work, but there was one more thing she wanted to check. Opening her social media app, she searched Kimberly's name for the latest news about her murder. Other than the reward going up, there wasn't any new information.

She heard the door to the restaurant open and turned around in her stool to watch a group of five come in. Whether she liked it her not, her break was almost over, and she had to be on her game for the rest of the evening. Normally, she didn't mind the short breaks and constantly being on her feet, but the stress and worry over Kimberly's case must have been bleeding into her working life, because she wasn't looking forward to getting back to work today.

Wanting to eke out as much of her break as she could, she scrolled through the social media app until she found the post about the reward for information about who killed Kimberly. She reread the comments from Noah and Carter, trying to see if she could pick out any new context now that she had met them. Nothing jumped out at her. Noah's comments indicated that he cared for Kimberly despite their breakup, but she didn't think that was too unusual. Ending a relationship didn't have to mean you hated the other person. She certainly wasn't in love with Jeremy anymore, but if *he* had been murdered, she would be deeply upset. That was just human.

She clicked on Noah's name, biting her lip as she navigated to the button that would let her send a message to him. She hadn't answered his questions the night before. In the dark, alone on an empty road, it had felt too dangerous. But maybe she *should* talk to him. Maybe telling him about the call would help. Maybe together, they could find answers.

Still undecided, she started typing out a message to him, trying to figure out how to word it. *I'm the woman who stopped to talk to you last night. I know more than I admitted then. Could we talk?*

She eyed the message critically, wondering if it made her sound like a serial killer. She probably shouldn't send it. Getting even more involved seemed like it had the potential to blow up in her face, but she couldn't stop thinking about Kimberly, and she didn't know where to turn next.

She was hovering between sending the message and deleting it when someone bumped her shoulder, making her thumb brush the screen right over the little arrow that would send the message to Noah. The message sent with a muted *whoosh*. She stared at the screen for a moment. The decision had been taken away from her, and her gut was screaming she shouldn't have sent that message.

Turning to see who had bumped into her, she realized the party of five that had come in a minute ago was trying to crowd into the bar area. She stood quickly, gathering her things and abandoning her seat. It was time to get back to work, no matter how distracted she was.

As she walked toward the kitchen, she felt her phone, still in her hand, buzz. Once she was through the doors and out of everyone's way, she paused to check it. It was a message from Noah. If he was surprised by her message, it didn't show.

When and where?

It was simple, short, and made it clear that she wasn't going to escape the consequences of her little mishap. Noah had her name now, and if he cared about what happened to his ex-girlfriend as much as she thought he did, he wasn't going to let this go.

ELEVEN

Thinking fast, Lydia typed out a response to Noah, asking if he could meet her at Iron and Flame just after ten. The kitchen closed at ten, but the dining room and bar were open until eleven. That meant they would have time to meet and talk somewhere that was somewhat public—and therefore, hopefully, safe—before her employees closed the restaurant for the night.

She had to focus on cooking after that and didn't get a chance to check her phone until nearly an hour later. When she did, Noah had responded, agreeing to meet. She felt a thrill of both nerves and anticipation. He had known Kimberly and had likely known her family too. If anyone knew more about her death than was available online, it would be him.

She did her best to focus on her job for the rest of the evening, and managed to avoid making any major mistakes, though she didn't completely lose herself in the act of cooking like she sometimes did.

She finished the last order—a filet mignon cooked medium rare with garlic green beans and their house mashed potatoes—a few minutes after ten and started cleaning up her workstation. She worked quickly, but still took the time to make sure everything was put away correctly. They had some very expensive appliances and tools in the kitchen, and the last thing she wanted was for one of her knives to rust or to scrub the seasoning off of her cast iron skillet just because she was in a hurry.

When she left the kitchen and entered the dining area, it only took her a moment to spot Noah. His brother, Carter, was with him, which she hadn't expected, though in retrospect, it made sense. He probably hadn't wanted to meet a complete stranger, especially one who had fudged the truth when asked about a murder, alone.

They were seated at a table near the back of the restaurant and had drinks and an appetizer in front of them, but no entrée. They must have come in just as the kitchen was closing. She thought she remembered seeing Chartreuse fry the mozzarella sticks a few minutes ago.

They both looked up as she approached the table, and Noah gave her a wary nod. Carter crossed his arms, looking at her skeptically.

"Thanks for meeting me here," she said as she sat down across from them. "My name is Lydia."

Noah introduced himself, then gestured at Carter, who grudgingly gave his name as well.

"Ignore him, he's just in a bad mood," Noah said.

"I think this is some sort of scam," Carter admitted. "I'm willing to listen, but like I told Noah, if you knew anything about her murder, you'd already have said something to the police. I don't like this."

"It's not a scam," she assured them. "And I did go to the police about this. I'm sorry for not being honest with you last night, but I was taken off guard." She took a deep breath. "Kimberly called me the night she was killed. She was trying to call her mother but got the number wrong and got me instead. I heard the last few minutes of her life, and until I know what happened, I won't be able to think about anything else."

She told them about the call in detail, then added, "I talked to her boss at the gas station, and I talked to her neighbor, Aiden, but neither of them had any idea who might have targeted her. I'm hoping there's been more progress on her case that people who were closer to her might be aware of."

She decided not to bring up the fact that Brandon had indicated his suspicion toward Noah. She didn't think it would help matters.

"Do you think if we had any idea who killed her, we would've been walking up and down that stretch of road in the middle of the night?" Noah asked. "No one has a clue who did it, and that's the problem. I could point fingers all day, but I don't have any proof about anything and neither does anyone else."

"So, you have a suspect, you just don't have any proof it was them?" she asked, desperate for any crumb of information.

Noah gave a bitter laugh and shrugged his shoulders. "Look, I loved Kimberly. Even after we broke up, I still cared for her well-being. But she was terrible at setting boundaries. I don't want to make it sound like she was leading people on, or like she deserved what happened to her, because she definitely didn't, but I do think she had a ... confused relationship with a lot of people. That's why I ended things with her. That neighbor of hers you said you talked to, Aiden? If you looked at them from the outside, you probably would've thought the two of *them* were dating. He gave her a ride to and from work every day, he brought her leftovers whenever he went out to eat, he had a key to her apartment and would walk in randomly, even while I was over, and he was constantly texting her. I might have been the only person she was being romantic with, but in every other way, it was like she was dating both of us. If you're asking me who my gut thinks did it, it's him. I had my suspicions that he was trying to break us up on purpose. I told her multiple times she needed to set some boundaries with him and with other people in her life, but she refused, and I had finally had enough."

Noah's face was red by the time he stopped talking, and he took a swig of his drink. It was obvious that the topic of Aiden bothered him deeply.

To Lydia's surprise, because he seemed more taciturn than his brother, Carter chimed in.

"It wasn't just Aiden she had problems with. I think her boss was crossing lines too. He was always asking her personal questions, and I know he kept offering her rides even after she turned him down. The fact that she turned him down should tell you how little she trusted him. He almost always scheduled their shifts together, too. We both told her we thought he was full of red flags and suggested that she start looking for a new job, but she wouldn't listen. We started taking turns stopping at the gas station whenever she was working to make sure she was okay. A secluded gas station, a creepy boss, and a girl who was more naïve than she should be…" He shook his head. "It was a disaster just waiting to happen, especially after she started walking home alone every night in the dark."

He shifted, his dog tags jingling, and grabbed one of the mozzarella sticks. He dipped it into the ramekin of marinara sauce with too much force, breaking it in half.

"It *could* have been Brandon," Noah agreed with a sigh as he watched his brother fish the marinara stick out of the sauce. "That's the thing, though. It could've been almost anyone. Maybe it was someone she knew, or maybe it was a complete stranger who drove past while she was walking home and thought she would make an easy target. She was one of the nicest people I've ever known. She didn't deserve to be strangled to death along a dark stretch of highway."

"She was strangled?" Lydia asked. She hadn't seen anything about *that* online. Was it a warning sign that Noah knew information the police hadn't released, or was she overthinking it?

"It's not public knowledge," Noah admitted. "Her parents told Carter it was her cause of death when they called to give us the news. I'm glad he took the call, because I don't think I could have handled it. I hate thinking about it. Part of me wonders if we will ever know what happened to her. I mean, it was the middle of nowhere. She was still in sight of the gas station, but only just, and she told me before that the cameras don't work. If no one witnessed her murder and her killer didn't leave any evidence behind, it seems like they might end up getting away with it."

It seemed hopeless to Lydia too. Still, maybe a miracle would happen. "Well, Brandon said that the outside security camera works intermittently," she said. "Maybe the police will get the warrant they need to search his computer, and they'll find footage that will tell us what happened."

"It does?" Carter asked.

"We can only hope it does," Noah said. "Are you sure you didn't hear anything when she called you? No voices?"

"I heard the sound of a couple cars driving by, but nothing else, other than her voice," Lydia said. "I'm sorry. I suppose I wasted your time by asking you to meet me here. I was hoping we could help each other."

"No, I'm glad you talked to us. It's good to know she wasn't completely alone at the end," Noah said somberly. "I'm glad you answered the phone, even if it was too late to help her."

Lydia blinked. She hadn't thought about it like that. She still felt like she had failed Kimberly, but maybe she had helped her a little more than she thought. Knowing she wasn't alone might have brought a tiny bit of comfort to her in her last moments. Maybe, just maybe, it was better than nothing.

TWELVE

Talking with Noah and Carter hadn't been as illuminating as she hoped it would be, but she felt like she had gotten a sort of closure from the conversation. Kimberly's death was still a mystery, but everyone; her family, friends, and Lydia alike, would have to accept that it might not get solved anytime soon, if at all. Focusing so much of her time and emotional energy on it was going to drive her crazy if there was no resolution, so she needed to make her peace with her grief and anger and focus on something else.

This somber acceptance stayed with her through the night and into the next morning, when she left to meet Lillian at Morning Dove for breakfast. Conversation with her sister was a little awkward, because Lydia wasn't sure she wanted to broach the subject of Kimberly yet, but it was still nice to see her. She would tell her sister eventually, but it wasn't even eight yet, which was too early to start the sort of argument she knew her revelation would entail.

Her sister must have scheduled her tire appointment for right when the auto shop opened, at seven-thirty on the dot, because her vehicle was ready for pickup by the time their check came. Feeling bad about keeping such a major event in her life from her sister, she invited Lillian to come for a late dinner after the kitchen closed at Iron and Flame that night.

"I'll whip up something for just the two of us," she said. "We'll have more time to talk then."

"That sounds amazing," Lillian said, giving her a quick hug before setting off down the sidewalk. "I'll see you later."

She resolved to catch her sister up on everything that had been happening in her life this evening. That was more than twelve hours away, though, and she had a whole day to get through first.

One last thing was bothering her about Kimberly's murder, and that was Brandon's reluctance to let the police search for video footage of the incident. She wondered if they had gotten their warrant yet, but she knew there was no way they would tell her if she tried to ask. She decided to go straight to the source. Brandon had seemed happy enough to chat the last time she was there, and she hoped he would be just as chatty today.

Making a mental promise to herself that this would be the last thing she did in regards to trying to solve Kimberly's murder, she drove north out of town along the highway, toward the gas station. Knowing that Kimberly had walked this route twice a day, every day made it feel longer, even though the drive was only a couple of minutes by car.

Her stomach dropped when she pulled into the gas station parking lot and saw that it looked closed. The neon open sign was turned off, there was no one parked at any of the pumps, and the interior lights were dim.

She checked the time, but it was nearly eight-thirty by now, and according to the sign on the door, the gas station opened at seven. Maybe the open sign was broken. It was a weak hope, but she decided to go with it, and pulled around back to the small parking lot. She didn't need gas and didn't want to take up a pump, though she doubted the gas station was going to suddenly get busy while she was inside.

An old sedan was parked in one of the spaces around the back, but it was the only vehicle there. At least *someone* was here. She parked beside the car and got out of her vehicle, keeping her keys in her hand as she jogged around to the front of the building.

She paused as soon as she rounded the corner. One of the big front windows was shattered, and the glass shards sparkled all over the pavement. She was shocked she hadn't noticed it before—now that she had seen it, she couldn't take her eyes off of the damage.

No wonder the gas station was closed at eight-thirty on a Tuesday morning. Someone had broken into it.

Dread washed over her as she realized just how wrong this was. Brandon—or whoever opened this morning—should have been here by now. She had seen another vehicle in the parking lot behind the building, so she knew *someone* was here. But if an employee had arrived to open the gas station only to find the broken window... Why wouldn't they have called the police? It had been nearly an hour and a half since this place was supposed to open, and she doubted it would take the police that long to respond. It was possible they had already come and gone, but there was no crime scene tape, and no sign anyone had started cleaning up the glass. The gas station looked deserted.

But that didn't mean it *was* deserted. What if the person responsible for the break-in was still inside?

Worse, what if whoever opened the gas station was inside and was hurt?

The second option had her taking a hesitant step forward. It would be smarter to stay out here and call the police, but her heart still insisted she hadn't done enough for Kimberly. What if there was someone in there who needed her help? She couldn't fail them too.

Drawing on every scrap of courage she could find—and ignoring the part of her brain that was telling her not to be an idiot—Lydia walked up to the door, her shoes crunching over the broken glass. She paused when her fingers closed around the door handle, wondering if it would be locked, but it opened easily when she pulled it. She stepped through the door as the electronic bell chimed. The sound was too loud against the silence of the store.

"Hello?" she called out. "Is anyone here?"

Silence. She looked around, but there was no sign that whoever broke the window had taken anything. The shelves looked untouched, and the cash register was still closed on the countertop. She took a few more hesitant steps in, when she paused again. Something had caught her eye.

A beige metal door with a printed sign that read *Employees Only* on it was half open, and there was an old fashioned, corded mouse on the floor in front of it.

Trying to keep her steps as silent as possible, she made her way toward the door. The lights were on in the room beyond, and she peered through the gap cautiously before pushing the door further open.

It looked like a break room. There was a ratty couch, a garbage can filled with empty chip wrappers and pop bottles, a coffee table with crumpled fast-food bags and half-empty drink containers on top of it, and in the corner, a computer screen and mechanical keyboard on a small desk. The rolling chair in front of it had been knocked over, and there was a cord dangling from the wall, not attached to anything. More cords traveled along the wall and ceiling, and when she backed up to follow their progress out of the breakroom, she saw that one went to the security camera behind the counter and the other went outside, presumably to the camera above the door.

She stared at the scene for a long moment, until, with lightning clarity, she understood what had happened. Someone had broken in and stolen the PC that the security cameras recorded their information to. This *had* to be related to Kimberly's murder. The thief hadn't taken anything else, at least not anything that was obvious.

The only question was ... who?

She backed out of the break room and turned toward the door, planning on locking herself in her

SUV and calling the police, but she stumbled to a stop after only a couple of steps, her eyes glued to a slumped form behind the counter.

She hadn't been able to see him from the door when she came in; the angle had been wrong. His body was hidden by the counter. But now, coming from the other direction, she could see Brandon sprawled out on the floor behind the counter. He had dark bruises around his neck and his eyes were open wide, bloodstained. It was clear that he wasn't breathing. She remembered what Noah said the evening before, about Kimberly having been strangled, and it only strengthened her conviction that whoever was behind the break-in and ... this ... was the same person who killed her.

Horrified, she took a step toward the body, but the sound of the electronic bell over the door dinging made her freeze. She glanced over as someone stepped through the door and into the gas station and saw not a hapless stranger hoping to buy gas, but someone she recognized. Someone she had seen only the night before.

Carter Robinson. He froze when he saw her, and neither of them moved a muscle for a long moment.

Finally, Lydia said, "I think someone broke in."

It was an inane thing to say, but her heart was pounding in her chest, and her mind was racing. She didn't know if Carter was innocent and had simply stopped to get gas or a snack at an inopportune time, or if he was returning to the scene of the crime for some unknown reason.

"Did you call the police?" he asked. He looked tense, but he wasn't looking at her. His eyes were darting around the store, as if he was looking for something.

Lydia started looking around the store too, wondering what it was he was trying to find. Was he looking for whoever had broken in, or something else?

"Not yet," she said, distracted. She mentally kicked herself. She should have said they were on their way. "I was just about to—" she started, inching toward the door, but broke off and froze mid-step when she spotted something out of place lying on the floor not far from Brandon's body.

Military dog tags and the broken chain that had held them. Her gaze immediately snapped up to Carter. His neck was bare.

Brandon must have torn the necklace off when his killer attacked him, and that killer was Carter. He met her gaze, then slowly moved his eyes down to the tags.

THIRTEEN

There was a single, endless moment where he stared at the tags, and she stared at him. When he moved, it was in the same instant Lydia did. He lunged for her as she turned and raced back toward the break room. He was faster than her, but she had a lead on him, and she slipped through the door and slammed it behind her before he reached her. She searched for a lock in a panic and found it just in time. The instant after she pressed the button, the door handle jiggled. A moment later, Carter started hitting the door, but it was made of metal, and it held.

The thudding stopped. Carter's voice came from the other side, low and dangerous. "Open the door right now, or it's going to go badly for you."

"I'm not going to do that," she replied. She took a deep breath and tried to keep her voice from shaking. "Why? Why did you kill Kimberly? It *was* you, wasn't it?"

There was another, sharper series of thuds, and she thought he was kicking the door. After what felt like a long time but was probably only a few seconds, he stopped again.

"I loved her," he said unexpectedly from the other side. "For a long time. I was friends with her first. We met in ninth grade; we had both just entered high school. We were best friends from the start. Noah was a year younger than us. She didn't even meet him until a year later. I knew right away that I was in love with her, but she always saw me as a friend. It was Noah, my *brother,* she started dating. Noah she was with all those years. I was always there in the background, a friend, but never anything more." He paused to take a breath. "Then, *finally,* they split up. I knew she was hurt Noah left her, but she would have been so much happier with me if she would just give it a chance. We were meant to be together. I came here every day to talk to her, to try to cheer her up, but she didn't want anything to do with me. She wouldn't even let me give her rides to work. I didn't want her walking alone." He gave a dry chuckle. "I thought it was dangerous."

"So, you killed her because she wasn't in love with you?" Lydia asked, anger suddenly replacing a portion of her fear.

"No," he said. His voice cracked as if he was truly upset. "I would've been content staying her friend forever, but that night … the night it happened … she told me to stop talking to her. She didn't want to see me anymore. She said I was being creepy and too intense, and that Noah was right, and she needed to start setting boundaries. She said she should have had that talk with me a long time ago." He paused for a moment. "All those years, I thought we had something special, even if it wasn't exactly what I wanted. I loved her, and all this time she was barely tolerating me. I wasn't planning on killing her, but when I followed her after she got out of work to try to talk her out of it, she started running away from me like she was afraid of me. Like she thought I was going to hurt her. Like all those years of friendship had never existed. Something inside of me snapped."

His voice had been growing steadily louder, and he kicked the door again as soon as he fell silent. Lydia jumped back. She felt sick, and her heart was in her throat, and she didn't know whether she wanted to scream or vomit. She glanced around the room for something that could help her, and realized there was a window behind the couch. Her car keys were still in her hand. If she could get out through the window, she could make it to her SUV and get out of here. She started backing toward the window but paused when she realized she had better keep him talking ... and keep him from wondering if the break room had another way out.

"And Brandon?" she said. "Why did you kill him?"

"You mentioned the video cameras last night, and the fact that one worked intermittently," Carter said as she started backing toward the window again. "So, I guess it was your fault. I couldn't take the risk that the camera had caught me waiting in the parking lot until she got out. I got here at six-thirty this morning and thought the place would be empty, so I broke in through the window, but Brandon must have decided to get an early start to the day. He recognized me, of course, and I couldn't let him call the police." He paused, and when he started talking again his voice was silky. "Listen, open the door and we can work this out. You seem like you're a reasonable woman. I'm sure we can come to an agreement."

Lydia shivered as she pulled the blinds open and unlocked the window. It opened with a squeak. She spent a handful of panicked seconds trying to figure out how to take the screen out, before she resorted to just shoving against it until it popped out of the frame with a clatter.

"What are you doing?" Carter said from the other side of the door.

She didn't bother answering him. Wincing as the window frame bit into her abdomen, she heaved herself through it and dropped to her hands and knees on the other side. Shoving herself to her feet, she sprinted the short distance to the SUV. She managed to hit the unlock button on her first try and got inside, slamming the door shut and smacking the button to lock it again. She didn't waste any time in starting the engine and peeling out of the parking spot, spitting gravel behind her. As she rounded the front of the building, she saw Carter coming through the front door, but he was too slow to stop her. She pulled onto the highway without even looking for oncoming traffic and raced toward town.

She knew without a doubt that Carter would kill her if he got the chance, but she wasn't going to give him one. If he tried to chase her, she would lead him straight to the police station, and if he fled, she had to believe they would catch him. She had done enough. All she could focus on right now was staying alive.

EPILOGUE

Lydia looked between the spider plant and the pothos. She wasn't sure which would look better hanging above the kitchen sink. It might not be a pet, but she thought a houseplant would go a long way toward cheering her house up. She just hadn't realized how many options there were.

It had been a week since she fled from Carter and spent four hours huddling in the police station until they tracked him down and arrested him, and she was still jumpy. Every time she saw someone coming toward her down the aisle, she felt a moment's fear it was him, but Carter was safely behind bars. He wouldn't be able to hurt anyone for a long time.

There would always be a part of her that wondered if she could have done more for Kimberly, but she was coming to terms with the fact that what happened to the other woman wasn't her fault. The whole experience had made her appreciate just how drama free her divorce with Jeremy had been, in retrospect. Sure, they had exchanged some angry words, but at least his brother hadn't ended up stalking and trying to kill her. There was a silver lining in everything.

She was reaching for the pothos when her phone buzzed with an incoming text message. She paused to check it and found a text message from Taylor.

Brunch with the girls next Wednesday. You're welcome to come. Bring a friend if you want; we already made reservations and we have a huge table!

She smiled as she typed out a response. It would be hard to face the entirety of her old friend group for the first time, but she was already looking forward to seeing them. She paused to think a moment before adding, *I might bring someone, I'll let you know*, to the end of her message.

She thought Valerie might like to go. She seemed like she would get along with the rest of the group, and it would be nice to see the other woman outside of Iron and Flame sometimes.

She sent the message and grabbed the pothos before she could change her mind, then turned her cart toward the registers.

She had done everything she could for Kimberly, and her life had to go on. She had a wonderful sister, forgiving friends, a job she loved—most of the time—and now she had a new houseplant to take care of. She was creating a new life for herself, and while she didn't know exactly where her journey was leading her, she was already happier than she had been before, and that was a sign she was on the right track.

Printed in Great Britain
by Amazon